# The Tree That Went For A Walk

The Tree That Went For A Walk

Garrett Summers

ILLUSTRATED BY

Grandma Tweetie Goose

For all those who need to know --
you are valuable. Just believe. G.S.

Baby Joe - I love you. G.T.G.

Every afternoon just before school let out, the tree by the old council hall woke up from his nap.

The happy tree would rustle his leaves and stretch his tip top branches, hearing a little creaking now and then as he stretched. Sometimes Blue, that friendly bluebird, would chirpy chirp as they both woke up. Blue lived in the tip top branches of the happy tree.

Blue and the happy tree enjoyed hearing the school children walk along the pathway under the tree shade.

Suddenly, a little girl skipped past whistling. She had just learned to whistle but was still working out how to snap her fingers.

The little girl had made a brightly colored pinwheel during art time. She skipped and she looked up and saw Blue singing in the tip top branches of the happy tree.

She was so happy being near the happy tree. She got on her tippy toes and she tucked her pinwheel gently in the bark of the happy tree.

"Oh how wonderful," said the happy tree who could not contain his excitement. His shimmery green leaves shinned brighter than ever before.

Blue sang excitedly and flew down to get a closer look at the pinwheel.

"Hurry up!" the little girl's brother called out. The little girl skipped away whistling as she skipped, trying her hardest to snap her fingers.

Blue and the happy tree decided that pinwheels are the best thing ever. The happy tree could not help it but his heart started to fill up with smiles.

He told Blue he was swelling with joy and his green leaves started delightfully shimmering and shimmering.

The next day as school let out Blue and the happy tree woke up and they got on their tippy toes to see if more pinwheels were coming. Their eyes grew as wide as they could stretch them.

A parade of delightful children waving balloons and pinwheels were headed their way!

Blue burst out in a delighted song while the happy tree shimmered his leaves excitedly.

They could see the little girl who skipped and whistled but this time she brought some friends too! She told her friends about the happy tree and Blue.

The joy being felt by the happy tree was not only shared by Blue but by the children as well.

As they arrived they gently tucked their pinwheels into the happy tree's bark as high as their tippy toes could reach.

The children skipped and felt full of joy.
The happy tree never felt so much joy.
Blue flew in loopy-tee-loops really fast.

She was so excited.

The happy tree decided being so full of joy is the best ever. He began to feel he could do just about anything when his heart was overflowing like this.

After the sun went down and the happy tree's friend the moon came up, the happy tree had a most excellent idea.

"Tomorrow, I am going to walk and skip and meet the school children," he said to himself.

"I am so joyful with my colorful pinwheels I believe I can do just about anything," he thought.

The next day as the happy tree woke up from his nap, he looked around and saw all of his pinwheels. "I can do it!" he said to Blue. "I AM going to walk and skip to the school," he said loudly.

The happy tree felt he could fly because his joy was so full. He got up on his tippy toes and watched for the children.

The happy tree began to feel waves of joy way down into his tree toes. The harder he believed he could skip the more full his joy became.

Then, ALL OF A SUDDEN!, he felt himself skipping. "Wow" he yelled!!

Blue darted in and out of the tippy top branches amazed at the happy tree.

"You are doing it!" Blue chirped excitedly as she darted in and out of the tippy top branches. The happy tree made it to the cool tall grass near the corner by the school yard and he stood still.

The happy tree was so joyful that ALL OF A SUDDEN blossoms popped out of his shimmering branches!

As the children came out of the school they ran up to their friend the happy tree. He was never more beautiful. His shimmering green leaves, heavy and full of colorful blossoms, created a beautiful canopy.

His pinwheels spun with excitement.

Blue sang her best trill song and flew her best loopy-tee-loops. The children were skipping around the happy tree when ALL OF A SUDDEN, a miracle happened. As they began to believe with their full joy they knew that they can do anything too!!

After the sun went down and their friend the moon came up, the happy tree, Blue and all the children started dreaming.

With their joyfulness spilling over as they were snuggled in their beds, they all agreed and understood that nothing was impossible.

They dreamed of new adventures and pinwheels, and whistling, and skipping, and canopies of blossoms, and balloons, and everything.

Anything beyond everything thing they could ever ask or think or imagine, they could have and do, when their joyfulness was overflowing.

About the Author

"Garrett Summers is from the Mohawk Nation, Bear Clan, and lives on the Six Nations of the Grand River, First Nations reserve, Ontario, Canada. He also enjoys a home in Southern California, where he was born. Garrett is a gifted writer and he believes we can all achieve our dreams when we are encouraged. He is a high school senior and headed to University to study Engineering.

Garrett has made it his mission, to improve the quality of life for those who may be struggling. He knows first hand how hard it is to manage a life-threatening condition.

Garrett wants to encourage children to embrace math and sciences early. He believes that every child can learn even the most difficult material. He believes if he can overcome and learn, anybody can. Garrett believes that STEM outreach to elementary and middle schools can make a difference in the quality of life for many, and he is going to use his books to help bridge the gap.

"Tomorrow's breakthroughs can start with the bright minds of our youngest children -- who are our gifts." G.S.

Garrett's next book is volume 1 of a new series that is in production now, The Adventures of Big G: The Zero Club.

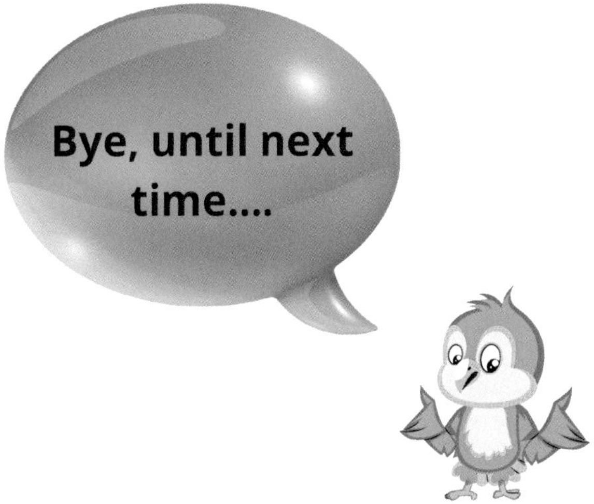
Bye, until next time....

Made in the USA
Middletown, DE
31 January 2022